The Boy with Flowers in His Hair

For Jenna

First US edition 2022

Library of Congress Catalog Card Number 2021947065
ISBN 978-1-5362-2522-8

22 23 24 25 26 APS 10 9 8 7 6 5 4 3 2

Printed in Humen, Dongguan, China

This book was typeset in Didot.
The illustrations were created digitally.

Candlewick Press
99 Dover Street
Somerville, Massachusetts 02144

www.candlewick.com

CANDLEWICK PRESS

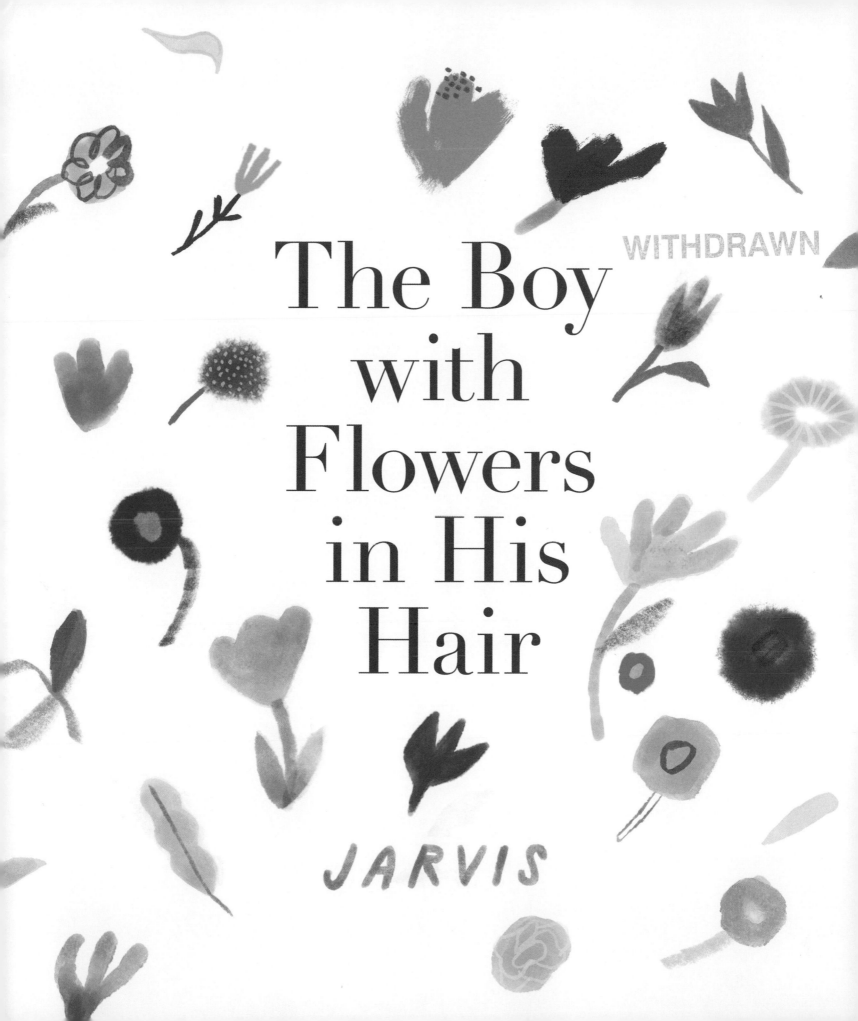

The Boy with Flowers in His Hair

JARVIS

His name is David.
He's the boy with flowers in his hair,
and he's my best friend.

Everybody likes David. Even Mrs. Jones,
and flowers make
her sneeze.

He's sweet and gentle. Just like his petals.

We have the best time together . . .

finding the
good puddles,

making up songs,

and running away
from the bees.

Once, he had a family of birds
living in his hair for a whole month.
It was really funny.

But one day, something happened.

I was watering David's hair
and one of his petals came off
in my hand.

That afternoon, he didn't want to play.

The next day, he started wearing a hat.
David never wore hats.

He was quiet.
David was *never* quiet.

Mrs. Jones asked us to take off our coats
and hats and scarves.

When David took off his,
petals fluttered down like butterflies.
David was twiggy, spiky, and brittle.

Everyone stayed away,
in case they got hurt by his branches.

I got a few scratches,
but it wasn't David's fault.

Then I had an idea.

I asked Mrs. Jones for a paintbrush ...

and some scissors,

and I found a way ...

to give David
his color back.

I made new flowers for David all the time.
Everybody wanted to help.

David seemed back to how he was before.

Almost.

Then, one day,
I noticed a different flower in David's hair.

It wasn't one of mine.
It wasn't one of anyone's.
It was David's.

It was a real flower,
a new flower,
prettier than ever.

More and more of David's own flowers started to bloom, and soon enough, all those buzzy bees were back!

So, right now,
David has lots and lots of flowers
in his hair.

But I'm making sure I still have
lots of paper ones just in case
he ever needs them.

Because he's my best friend,
and I am his.